CHE

PUZZLES

David Norwood

Edited by Lisa Watts and Carol Varley
Designed by Fiona Brown
Illustrated by Ian Winter

Additional illustrations by Susannah English

With thanks to Frank Van Hasselt

Contents

Thank you to Peter Wells, Talal Ja'bari, Tim Barker, Sam Pickles and James Thacker for checking the puzzles in this book.

Susannah English is represented by the Steven Wells Illustration Agency.

First published in 1991 by Usborne Publishing Ltd., Usborne House, 83-85 Saffron Hill, London EC1N 8RT, England. © 1991 Usborne Publishing Ltd. The name Usborne and the device 🐝 are Trade Marks of Usborne Publishing Ltd.
All rights reserved. No part of this publication may be reproduced, stored in a retrieval system, or transmitted in any form or by any means, electronic, mechanical, photocopying, recording or otherwise, without prior permission of the publisher.
Printed in Portugal.

Using this book

Working on the puzzles in this book will help you to improve your chess skills, giving you lots of practice in finding solutions for tricky chess positions that may occur in your games. The puzzles at the beginning of the book are easier than those later on, so working through the earlier puzzles will help you to build up the experience you need to tackle the more difficult ones.

Following the puzzles

Each puzzle is illustrated with a chess board using the piece symbols shown on the right. Chess moves are indicated by red or green arrows on the boards, as shown below.

The moves are written in algebraic notation, which is explained on page 64. There is also a glossary on pages 62-63, where you can look up chess terms used in this book.

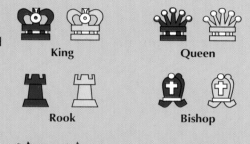

King	Queen
Rook	Bishop
Knight	Pawn

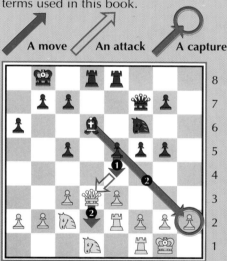

A move **An attack** **A capture**

Answers, clues and tips

Some of the puzzles have clues to help you spot key features. These puzzles are marked with the symbol shown on the right. The clues are on pages 40-43.

The puzzle answers, along with detailed explanations can be found on pages 44-61.

There are Puzzle Master tips on many pages too, giving general hints on how to improve your puzzle-solving skills.

Solving the puzzles

You may be able to solve some of the easier puzzles just by studying the diagrams in the book, but for the more difficult puzzles, you will need to set up the position on a chess board.

Some of the puzzles are real brainteasers, so it is a good idea to set up the position and keep returning to it when you have a new idea, or discuss it with friends.

Do not worry, though, if you cannot solve all the puzzles. It can be just as satisfying to study the answer and follow it on your chess board.

Pawn puzzles

The Pawn is the weakest piece, but if a Pawn reaches the other end of the board it can be promoted to a Queen or any other piece. At the beginning of the game, Pawns usually move out to open the lines and defend the centre of the board. Later on, they become more active.

1

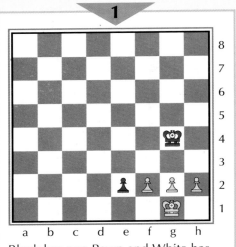

Black has one Pawn and White has three, but Black's Pawn is more powerful. Can you see why?

2

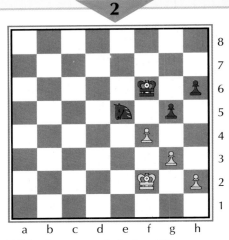

White has a good chain of Pawns that can support each other. What is White's strongest move?

3

This diagram shows all the possible moves for the White Pawn on g2. Which do you think is the best move: **1.g3**, **1.g4** or **1.gxh3**?

4

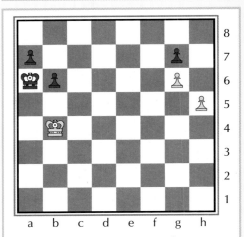

White, to move, is a Pawn down, but can win by promoting a Pawn. Which of the two Pawns can White promote in three moves?

Knight puzzles

The Knight can hop over pieces, so it is mobile early in the game. It can also stage surprise attacks from behind other pieces. The Knight is more powerful in the centre of the board, from where it can move to more squares, than when it is placed near the edge of the board.

1

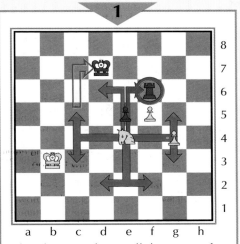

This diagram shows all the moves for the White Knight on e4. Which is the best move?

2

White has a very powerful move that wins an important piece. Can you spot White's move?

3

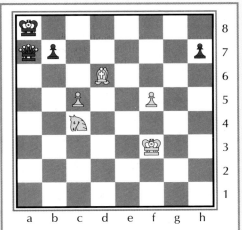

Can you spot a move for the White Knight that will allow White to win an important piece next turn?

4

Black has no Queen but the Black Knight can give mate in two different ways. Can you find both ways?

Bishop puzzles

In general, the Bishop is as valuable as the Knight, but it cannot hop over other pieces so it can be clumsy in closed positions. On open lines, though, the Bishop can dominate the game for, unlike the Knight, it can sweep from one side of the board to the other.

1

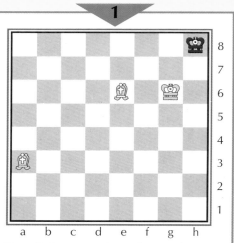

Two Bishops can be a devastating force. Here, they have driven the King into a corner and are ready for mate. Can you see how?

2

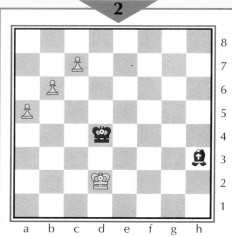

Black is in trouble. White's Pawns are very close to promoting. Can you find a way for Black to save the game and force a draw?

3

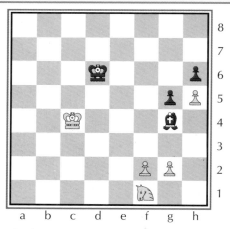

Black is a Pawn down but can come back with a vengeance. Can you spot Black's best move?

4

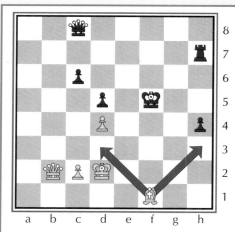

The White Bishop can make two good moves: **1.Bh3+** or **1.Bd3+**. Which would you choose?

Rook puzzles

A Rook is more powerful than either a Knight or a Bishop. In an endgame when there are no other pieces on the board, a King and a Rook can mate an enemy King, whereas a King and Knight, or King and Bishop, cannot. Rooks are most powerful on open lines.

1

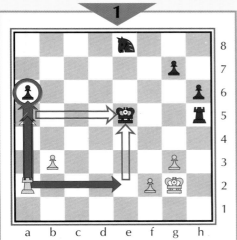

White is a Knight down, but has a strong Rook that can move along open lines. Which is the best Rook move: **1.Re2+**, **1.Ra5+** or **1.Rxa6**?

2

The Black King has a Knight to defend it, but White can win the Knight in three moves. Can you see how? White to move.

3

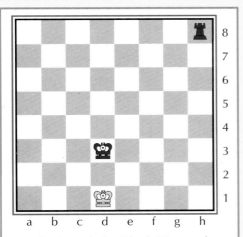

On this board, the Black King and Rook are about to mate the enemy King. Can you see how?

4

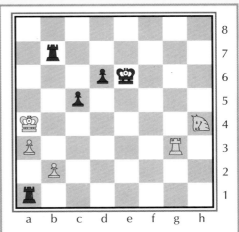

Here, White is confronted by two enemy Rooks and Black has a very strong move. Can you spot it?

Queen puzzles

The Queen is the most mobile piece on the board, and a powerful attacking piece. Like the Bishop, it can sweep along diagonals and, like the Rook, it can move horizontally and vertically. This is why players choose to promote a Pawn to a Queen in most cases.

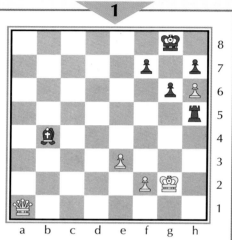

The Queen is a good piece with which to play for mate. Here, White can finish off Black with one move. Make sure you choose the right one.

The White Queen can check the Black King in many ways – and take a piece each time. How many ways can you see?

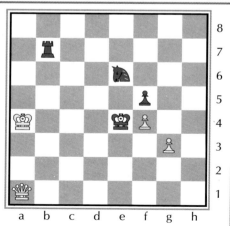

White can check the King and then win the Knight or Rook – but only one can be taken safely. Which one?

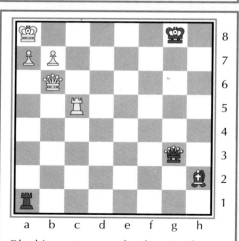

Black's next move checkmates the White King. What is Black's mating move?

King puzzles

Usually, you should guard your King, but sometimes, especially in the endgame, you can use the King more actively to help give checkmate and win material.

Puzzle Master tip

● The King is usually safest when surrounded by its own pieces, but be careful not to block your King's escape squares.

1

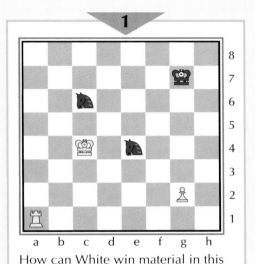

How can White win material in this position?

2

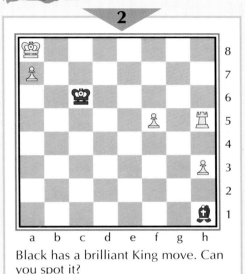

Black has a brilliant King move. Can you spot it?

3

Here, White can give checkmate in one move – you need to think carefully about this one.

4

This is a tricky one. Can you find a two-move mating sequence for White? White to move.

Checkmate in one

In the puzzles on these two pages you have to find a way to deliver mate in one move. There are some general tips to help you on the opposite page and there are clues to specific puzzles on page 40.

1

Just in case you think mate in one is too easy, the position above is from a game in which a Grandmaster missed White's winning move. Can you find it?

2

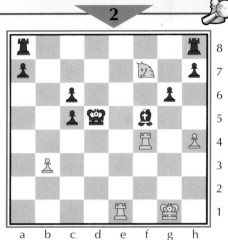

In this game played by our author, David Norwood, and a Russian Grandmaster, Norwood (Black) played **1…Kd5**, and was shocked by White's reply. What was it?

3

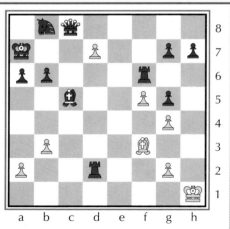

On this board, whoever moves, wins. Can you spot a mate for Black and one for White?

4

The Black King looks vulnerable, but there is only one way to finish Black off. What is it?

5

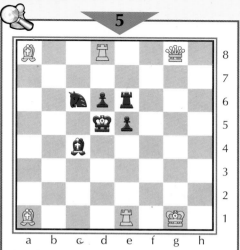

On this board, White can use the pin attack to great advantage. Can you spot White's mate?

6

Black has some good moves on this board. Can you spot the tactic that finishes the game immediately?

Puzzle Master tips

● Consider all possible moves – the most brilliant solutions are often the least obvious ones.

● When planning mate, try to cut off all the enemy King's escape squares.

● Look out for skewers, forks and pins to use to your advantage.

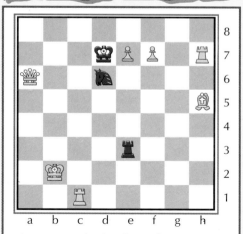

There is no doubt about the outcome of this game, as White has a much stonger army than Black. But finding mate in one move is not easy for White. Can you spot it?

7

In this game, White, a young chess star, was mated in the opening. White greedily captured the Black Bishop on b4. How did Black teach White a lesson?

8

Two-move mates

In each of these puzzles you need to think a little further and find a sequence of two moves that leads to mate. After the first move and your opponent's reply, your second move should give checkmate.

1

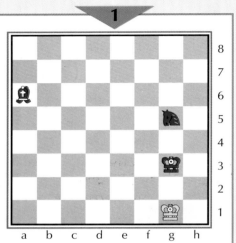

Here, Black can checkmate the White King in the corner in just two moves. Black to move.

2

Black is in trouble. How can the White Knights be used to deliver checkmate? White to move.

3

Both sides have the same pieces and the Pawn structure is symmetrical, but White's Rooks are better placed on open lines. How can White deliver mate in two?

4

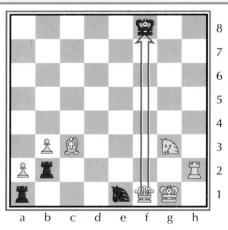

Here, Black is in check – but remember, moving the King is not always the best escape from check. How can Black go on the attack and give mate in two?

This tricky puzzle is taken from a real game situation. Can you spot White's brilliant two-move mate?

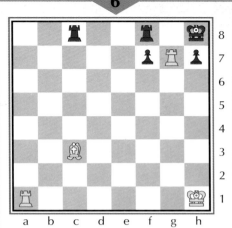

Here, White has an extra Bishop, but there is only one way for White to mate in two. What is it?

DID YOU KNOW?

● The first chess problem ever to be published was called the "Indian" problem. It appeared in *The Chess Player's Chronicle* in 1845.

● One of the most frustrating chess puzzles ever invented was composed in 1822 by J.N. Babson. In this puzzle, White, to play, has to deliver mate in 1,220 moves.

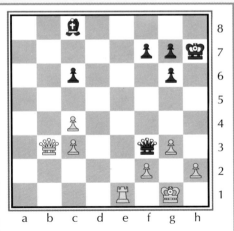

On this board, White has *fianchettoed* in front of the King and then lost the *fianchetto* Bishop. How can Black use this situation to deliver mate in two?

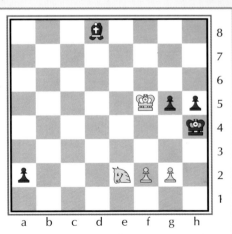

Combinations which require simple moves are often the hardest to spot. Here, White's position looks desperate, but with a sharp eye you could save it. White to move.

More two-movers

The puzzles on these two pages are a little more difficult. In the four below, you do not know whose move it is. On each board, either

Black or White is about to mate the enemy King in two moves. If you get stuck, turn to the clues on page 40 to find out whose move it is.

1

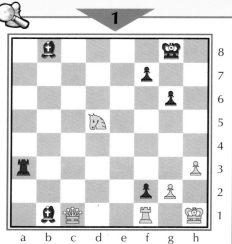

On this board, White still has a Queen, while Black has a powerful pair of Bishops. Which of the two can bring about a two-move mate?

2

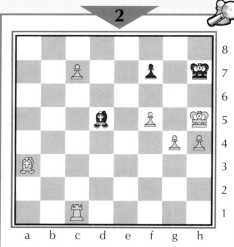

White certainly has more pieces – an extra Rook and three Pawns – but are you sure it is White and not Black who has the mate?

3

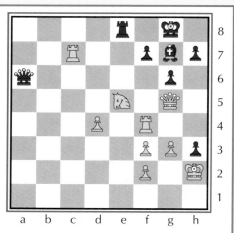

Black is a Rook down but has a strong Queen. Who do you think can win on this board?

4

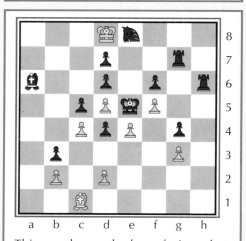

This puzzle may look confusing – but remember, it is often the most innocent-looking move that is best.

Two moves – two solutions

This time you are told which side can give mate in two, but each puzzle has two solutions, that is, the winning side can mate in two different ways.

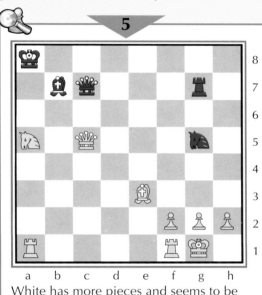

White has more pieces and seems to be doing well, but Black has two different ways to deliver mate in two. Can you find them?

Puzzle Master tips

● When trying to find mate, look at the enemy King's escape squares and decide which of your pieces are attacking, or can attack, those squares.

● If your opponent's pieces are blocking their own King's escape squares, see if you can use this to your advantage.

● Try to ensnare the enemy King in a position where the King is trapped by pieces of either colour. You can then move in to attack the King and deliver mate.

DID YOU KNOW? The Queen and Bishop were not introduced into the game of chess until 1475. For some time, the new game was sneeringly called the "mad Queen" version, until people realized how much more exciting it was.

White has two strong mating combinations – one of which involves a sacrifice. Can you spot the two different ways in which White can give mate in two moves?

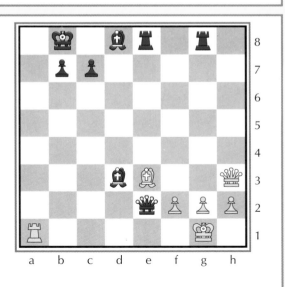

Tactics and combinations

Before you can deliver mate, you usually need to weaken your opponent's army by winning pieces. In these puzzles, see if you can win material with a two- or three-move combination. Look out for pins, skewers, sacrifices and other tactics to use to your advantage.

1

How does the awkward placing of Black's King and Rooks allow White to win an important piece in three moves? White to move.

2

White has played **1.Bb4**, pinning Black's Queen. Can you spot a three-move combination for Black that leaves Black a Pawn and Bishop up?

3

Can you find a clever combination which will win a Pawn for Black? Black to move.

4

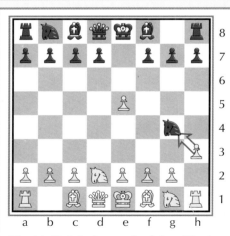

Black's Knight is attacked, but Black is only too willing to move it. What is Black's winning combination?

White is behind on material (White has 8 points, Black has 11), but White can gain the material advantage by sacrificing a piece. Can you spot White's tactical two-move ploy? (For more about point values, see page 63.)

Black's Pawn on e3 is close to promoting, but if Black plays **1...e2**, White can stop the Pawn with **2.Re7**. Can you spot a different combination for Black that leaves White helpless to stop the Pawn promoting?

In this Rook and Pawn endgame, the Black Rook has lined up behind the White a-Pawn in an attempt to stop it from promoting. Can you find a tactical three-move combination for White that leaves White a Rook up?

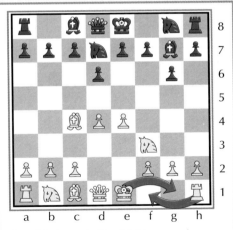

On this board, David Norwood, our author, had Black and was happy to see his opponent castle. He realized that White had missed an excellent chance to win material and open up the defences around the Black King. What was it?

Sacrifice to win

No one likes to lose a piece, but sometimes it can be well worth your while. In the puzzles on these two pages, you again have to work out how to mate the enemy King in two moves. This time, though, it is not possible to achieve mate without making a sacrifice.

1

White is two pieces down, having lost both Bishops. Can you see how White can sacrifice a piece to deliver mate on the second move?

2

The White King is defended by only a thin line of Pawns. Can you spot a sacrifice for Black that leads to mate on the second move?

3

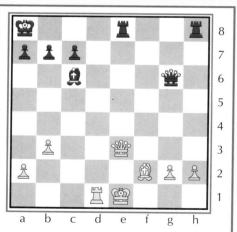

In this puzzle, White can sacrifice a piece to free another piece to deal the final blow. Can you see how?

4

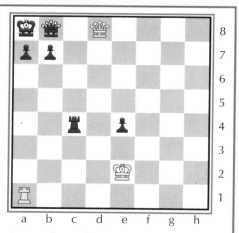

Our author, playing White, was three Pawns down but he had a winning sacrifice. Can you spot it?

5

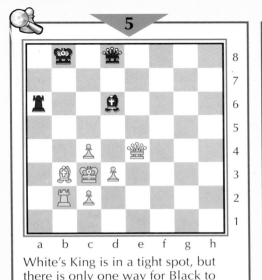

White's King is in a tight spot, but there is only one way for Black to mate in two and it involves a sacrifice. Black to move.

6

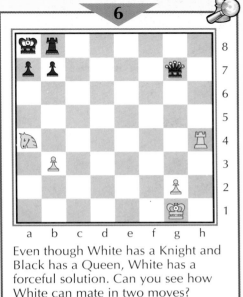

Even though White has a Knight and Black has a Queen, White has a forceful solution. Can you see how White can mate in two moves?

DID YOU KNOW? The game of chess has a ruling goddess called Caissa. She was first introduced in a poem by Sir William Jones in 1763, where she is described as a beautiful nymph, admired and pursued by the great god Mars. In the poem, Mars invents the game of chess in an attempt to win Caissa's heart.

7

White can trap Black in a smothered mate. Which piece should White sacrifice, and what are the two moves to mate?

8

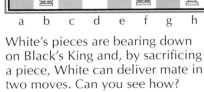

White's pieces are bearing down on Black's King and, by sacrificing a piece, White can deliver mate in two moves. Can you see how?

Study puzzles

In chess terminology, a study is a chess position that has been set up to create a challenging puzzle. Studies are quite difficult and require all your chess skills. There are some tips to help you below.

Puzzle Master tips

Because a study has been specially designed as a puzzle, the pieces are often in an unusual arrangement that is unlikely to occur in an actual game. Studies also tend to have unusual or even bizarre solutions – for example, it is often a humble Pawn or an oddly positioned piece that actually delivers mate. Studies are therefore a good way to practise lateral thinking when approaching chess problems. Here are some tips for solving studies.

● First, from the arrangement of the pieces, identify that the problem is probably a study and be prepared to look for an unusual solution.

● Study the position of each piece – it has been placed there for a particular reason. Look carefully at any piece whose role is not so obvious, as it may be the key to the answer.

● Try to work out the mating net, or the square on which the King could be mated, then work backwards to see how the mate could be brought about. (For more practice in solving puzzles by working backwards, see Retro-puzzles, pages 28–29.)

● Be cunning. Studies require skilful manoeuvres rather than obvious attacking or checking moves. For example, a placid waiting move may cause the enemy King to become trapped among its own pieces.

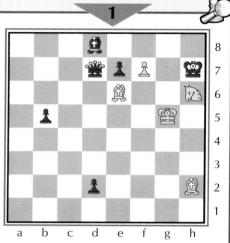

Here, White can capture the Queen or promote a Pawn, but for White to mate in two, a more unusual solution is required.

White is winning and the logical move is to save the Rook on a2. Instead, White can attack and reach mate in two. Can you see how?

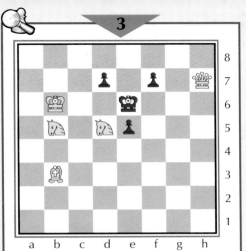

White has to play a peculiar move to force mate in two – moving a piece away from an attacking position and leaving another piece unprotected. How can White complete the mating net around the King and force mate in two?

White's most obvious moves are with the major pieces but, in fact, a quiet move by the White King is the key to the solution. Again, try to deliver mate in two by completing the mating net around the Black King and cutting off its escape squares.

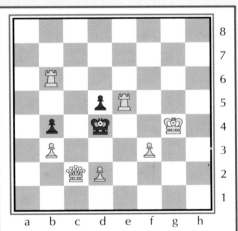

This is a difficult study. For White to mate in two, you need to find a quiet move that will put Black in *zugzwang*, so that whatever Black does, mate is inevitable. As in Puzzle 3, you need to move a piece away from an attacking position so that White can deliver mate on move two.

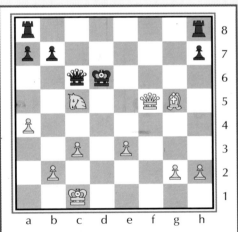

Although the position on this board looks as though it could have been designed as a study, it occurred in one of the author's games. David Norwood, playing White, was unable to find a mate in two. Can you spot the move that leads to mate the following move?

Save yourself puzzles

Sometimes your position is so bad that the best you can aim for is a draw – a way to avoid losing the game. There are two obvious ways of doing this – with perpetual check or stalemate. Can you save yourself in the puzzles on these two pages?

Ways to draw

● Perpetual check is a position where a King cannot escape constant checks.

● In stalemate, the player whose turn it is to move next can make no legal move, but is not in check. You can force stalemate by positioning your pieces so that your opponent's moves leave *you* with no legal reply, or you can try to create a position where *your opponent* has no legal move.

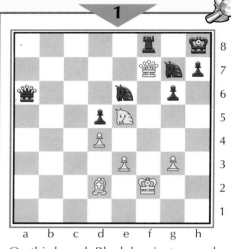

On this board, Black has just moved the Rook to f8 and expects White to resign. It is possible, however, for White to force a draw. Can you see how?

This puzzle has two parts:
a) White is a Queen, a Bishop and two Pawns down, yet can salvage a draw. Can you see how?
b) Now imagine the position without the Pawn on e5. Can White still force a draw?

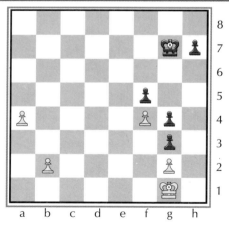

Black is in trouble. The White a-Pawn is advancing up the board and the Black King cannot catch it before it promotes. Can you see how Black, in four moves, manages to create a position which is a draw? Black to move.

2

3

The position shown on the board below is from a game played in 1958 by Khalomoyez and Gurin, two Soviet Masters, in Simferopol, in the Soviet Union. Gurin, playing Black, saw that his Pawn was attacked and decided to push it to g1 and promote it.

The Pawn can be promoted to a Knight, Bishop, Rook or Queen. You might think that Black could not help but win with so many options. White, however, has a good defence whichever piece Black chooses – and, in some cases, can even win.

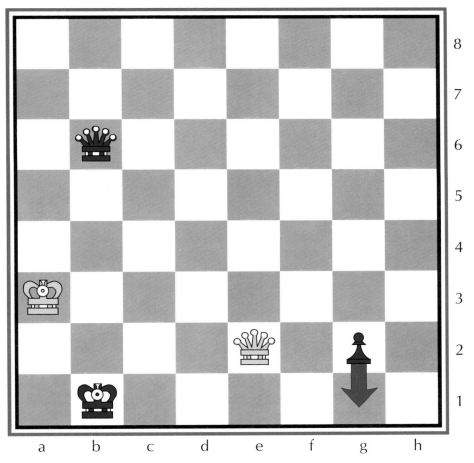

For each piece to which the Pawn can be promoted (the options are shown below), what is White's defence, and in each case, how will the game end?

a) Pawn to Knight

b) Pawn to Bishop

c) Pawn to Rook

d) Pawn to Queen

Advanced winning techniques

So far, most of the puzzles have involved combinations of one or two moves. But to become a Puzzle Master you must be able to think a little deeper. In the following problems you need to find mating combinations of three or four moves.

With longer combinations it is impossible to analyse every possible move – there are too many. Instead, look for a winning strategy, such as those listed in the tips below.

Puzzle Master tips

● Look at your own position before you go on the attack. Are you in danger yourself? If your opponent has a mating move, your first priority is to prevent this.

● Examine the position of the enemy King. Does it look exposed or trapped, perhaps on the back rank? Can you lure, rather than force, the enemy King into a mating net?

● Look for pieces to sacrifice to improve your position or trap the enemy King.

● Can you win material with a tactical trick such as a check, pin, skewer or fork?

● Look for forcing moves, such as checks, that leave your opponent with only a limited number of replies. It is easier to plan long combinations if you can predict your opponent's responses.

This position is from a game played in 1852 between two German world class players: A. Anderssen and J. Dufresne. Anderssen, playing White, spotted a brilliant mating combination. Can you find a mate for White in three or four moves? White to move.

1

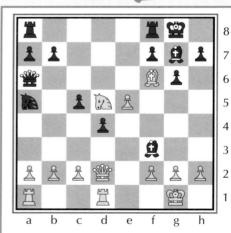

It is White's move and many a strong player would play **1.gxf3**. A Puzzle Master, though, would realize that the White Bishop and Knight are ready to attack the King and that a mate may be in sight. Can you find the devastating move for White that leads to mate in up to four moves?

2

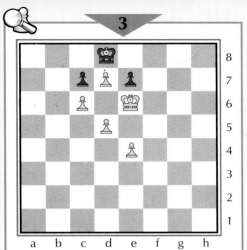

This is a tricky puzzle. White, with two extra Pawns, is winning, and your task is to mate Black in four moves. It is White's move and the main problem is to avoid putting Black in stalemate. If you can keep Black on the move, you should be able to deliver mate in four. Be careful not to give Black too much freedom, though.

Black's King is exposed and the Black Queen and the Rook on a7 are blocked and out of play. White can deliver mate in four moves, but to find the mating combination you need to spot clever Queen moves for White on moves two and three. Move two is an ordinary check and move three threatens mate in two different ways. White moves first.

This position is taken from the chess notebook of an Italian Master, Damiano, and dates from 1512. Can you find White's three-move mating combination? White to move.

Black has a winning move, to which White can reply in various ways. Analyse White's defences carefully to find a mate for Black in up to four moves. Black to move.

Help-mate puzzles

In the puzzles on these two pages, the aim is not to defeat your opponent but to defeat yourself! You have to find a sequence of moves that will enable your opponent to mate you. Many of the world's leading Grandmasters claim that composing and solving help-mate puzzles helps them to play better chess.

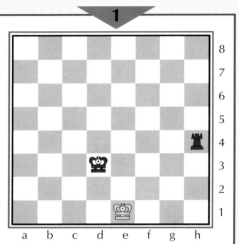

Here is an easy example to start with. White, to move, has a help-mate in one. That is, in one move, White moves to a position where Black can give checkmate. Can you spot White's move?

This puzzle is a little harder but you still only need to think one move ahead. White, to move, has a help-mate in one. Can you see a move for White that allows Black to achieve checkmate next move?

In this puzzle, White has a help-mate in two: White plays a move, Black replies, White plays another move and Black delivers checkmate. Black has only a King and a Knight, and an endgame with a King and a Knight against a lone King is always a draw. On this board, though, White also has a Rook – and that makes all the difference. Can you see how Black, with White's help, is able to deliver mate on the second move? White to move.

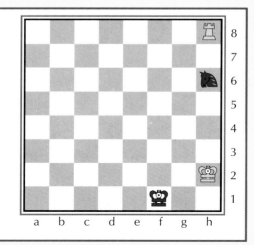

4

In this position, Black has a help-mate in three. To deliver checkmate, White has to make active use of both the King and the Rook. The trick is to try to move the White King on to a useful square while manoeuvring the Black King on to a vulnerable one. Black to move.

5

On this board, White has a help-mate in five. But do not worry – long puzzles are not always the most difficult. In this puzzle, once you have worked out how to drive the White King to a vulnerable square, delivering mate is quite easy. White to move.

Puzzle Master tips

● Decide which squares are attacked by the mating side's pieces and try to organize the pieces to form a mating net.

● Look for a vulnerable square for your King – a corner for example, or near the edge of the board.

● Remember, one of the most common mates is a back rank mate, where the King is trapped on the first rank by its own pieces. Can you manoeuvre the pieces to trap your King?

This puzzle is quite difficult. White has a help-mate in three. The trick is to imagine a position in which White can be mated, and the first thing to notice is that the Black King is too far away to help. Can you find a way for the Black Rook, on its own, to mate the White King? White to play.

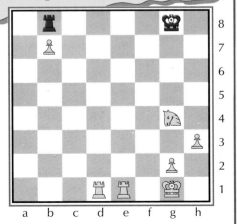

6

Retro-puzzles

Retro means backwards, and in these puzzles you have to be a detective and work out what has happened in the game so far. By observing which pieces have moved and which have been captured, you can deduce which moves might have taken place. But be careful, in retro-puzzles, things are not always as simple as they seem...

1

On the board below, your task is to work out which piece, or pieces, could have captured the Black Knight. To find this out, you need to decide what has happened on the board up until now.

In fact, very little appears to have happened. All you can say with certainty is that the White Bishop and Black Knight have been captured, and that the Bishop must have been taken on a6 by the b7 Pawn. You can be sure of this because Pawns do not lie. A Pawn cannot move backwards and if a Pawn has moved diagonally, it must have made a capture. Black's doubled Pawns on a6 and a7 show that a capture must have taken place, and the Bishop is the only White piece that is missing.

But what about the Black Knight? You may be tempted to think that the Black Knight was captured on a6 by the Bishop, and the Bishop was then taken by the Pawn – but you have no proof. The Knight could, for example, have been taken by the White Queen, which then returned to its own square, while the Bishop voluntarily moved to a6 and was captured by the Pawn.

Now, remembering that Pawns do not lie, can you deduce which pieces might, according to the rules of chess, have captured the Black Knight?

Puzzle Master tip

In retro-puzzles, forget about the probable and think about the possible.

Who took the Black Knight?

Did the White Queen capture the Knight?

Could the King have captured the Knight?

Are the Bishops guilty?

Could the Rooks have moved?

One day, Mr White and Mrs Black visited their local chess club and sat at a table in the corner. On this table there was a chess board, on which the position shown on the board below had been reached by two young players. The players had abandoned their game so Mr White and Mrs Black decided to take up where they had left off.

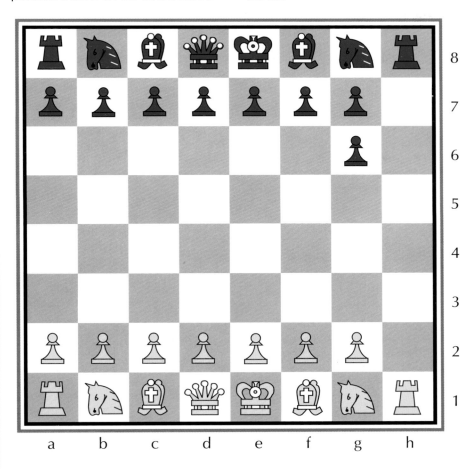

Mr White chose White and Mrs Black chose Black and the game continued until Mr White decided to castle. At this point, Mrs Black protested that White could not castle.

"Can't castle?" grumbled Mr White.

"It's not allowed," said Mrs Black. "You've already moved your Rook, the one on h1."

"I have?" said Mr White. "How do you know?"

"Look at the position with which we started," replied Mrs Black. "It couldn't have been reached without any Rook moves."

Was Mrs Black right? Has the Rook on h1 already moved or not? And if it has, how did you work it out?

Brainteasers

Here are some slightly unusual puzzles to test your chess skills. Working on unorthodox studies like these helps to improve your problem-solving skills by encouraging you to think of unusual solutions.

1

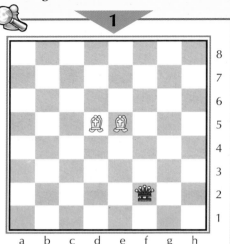

Of course, this board position could not be from a real game – there are no Kings. Your task is to place the Kings so that White, to move, puts Black in checkmate. Try to find the most vulnerable square for the Black King and position the White King so it can deliver mate with the help of the two Bishops.

2

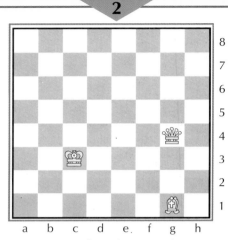

Here is a another classic study. On this board, your task is to find three different positions for the Black King. See if you can place the King so that it is:

a) in checkmate.
b) in stalemate.
c) about to be mated by White's next move.

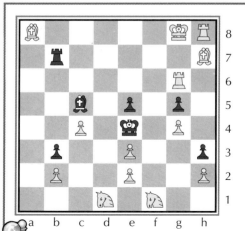

DID YOU KNOW? Many movie stars have been chess enthusiasts – John Wayne, Charles Chaplin, Marlon Brando and Humphrey Bogart to name but a few.

In this puzzle, you have to find a way for White *not* to deliver mate. It seems that every move White can make puts Black in checkmate. Can you find the one White move that keeps Black in the game?

3

● William the Conqueror once broke a chess board over his opponent's head. This weapon was used by a French knight, Renaud de Montauban, with even more dramatic effect – he killed his opponent.

● In 1914, a German chess magazine reported a particularly tricky retro-puzzle. The solver was given a board position and had to work out whose move it was next. The only way to find the answer was to work backwards 53 moves to the beginning of the game.

CHESS QUOTES

"Chess is a fine entertainment."
Leo Tolstoy

"Chess is too difficult to be a game, and not serious enough to be a science or an art." *Napoleon Bonaparte*

"Chess is life." *Bobby Fischer*

"Chess is vanity."
Alexander Alekhine

"Chess is a sad waste of brains."
Sir Walter Scott

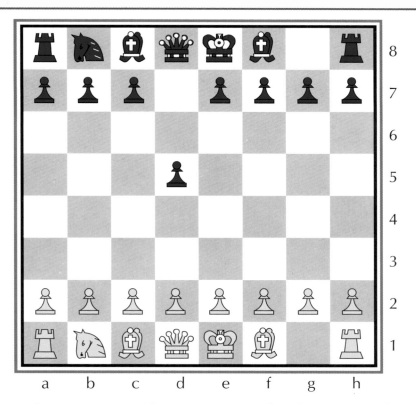

This puzzle requires some of the retro-analytical skills that you used in the puzzles on the previous two pages. Each side has played just four moves. Can you work out what they were? In fact, there are several possibilities, all leading to the position shown above, with Black and White both losing a Knight. White moves first.

4

Mate the Grandmaster

All these positions are from real game situations in which a Grandmaster was, or could have been, checkmated. Imagine you are a world class Master and see if you can checkmate the Grandmaster.

1

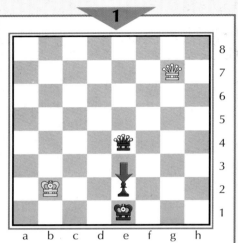

This board is from a game between two Soviet Masters, Babuyev and Smagin, played in Riga, in 1954. Smagin, playing Black, has just advanced his Pawn to e2 and is expecting victory. If you were playing White, how would you checkmate him?

2

This position is from a game between Frazekas and Speelman in 1938. White's position looks hopeless: his Queen is threatened and Black is also threatening to capture the Pawn on f2. If you were in Frazekas's place, playing White, would you resign or find a better solution?

3

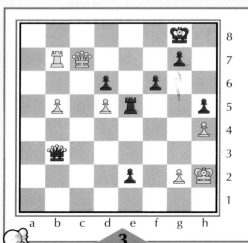

INDIAN PROVERB   Chess is a sea in which a gnat may drink and an elephant may bathe.

This position is from Tolush-Keres, Leningrad, 1939. Paul Keres, one of the best players of his day, wanted to promote his Black Pawn but was threatened by White playing **1.Qxg7++**. Can you spot the brilliant sequence that Keres found to promote the e-Pawn and deliver mate? Black to move.

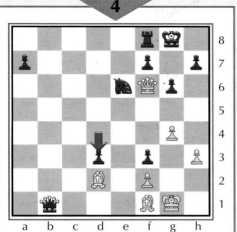

4

In this position from Havana, 1965, Boris Ivkov, one of the world's leading Grandmasters, was playing against Gilbero Garcia, a relatively unknown Cuban player. Ivkov is Black and has been winning easily for most of the game. However, his last move, Pawn to d3, was a terrible blunder. How would you, playing White, deliver mate?

5

Here is your chance to checkmate Korchnoi, the famous World Champion contender. This position is from Korchnoi-Karpov in the 1978 World Championship match. Korchnoi has just moved a Rook to a1, one of the worst moves of his career. Can you find how the World Champion, playing Black, mated Korchnoi in just three moves?

World Champions

W. Steinitz	(Bohemia/USA)	1886–94
E. Lasker	(Germany)	1894–1921
J. Capablanca	(Cuba)	1921–27
A. Alekhine	(USSR/France)	1927–35
M. Euwe	(Holland)	1935–37
A. Alekhine	(USSR/France)	1937–46
M. Botvinnik	(USSR)	1948–57
V. Smyslov	(USSR)	1957–58
M. Botvinnik	(USSR)	1958–60
M. Tal	(USSR)	1960–61
M. Botvinnik	(USSR)	1961–63
T. Petrosian	(USSR)	1963–69
B. Spassky	(USSR)	1969–72
B. Fischer	(USA)	1972–75
A. Karpov	(USSR)	1975–85
G. Kasparov	(USSR)	1985–

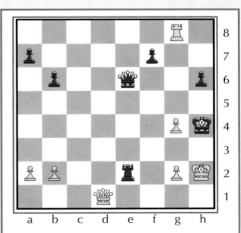

This position is taken from a game between Ståhlberg and Becker, in Buenos Aires, 1944. How would you, playing White, end the game quickly? White to move.

6

Puzzle Master Quest

You have tackled many puzzles and now you should be prepared to face the final challenge – the Puzzle Master Quest. You will encounter six different characters: a Pawn, a Knight, a Bishop, a Rook, a Queen and a King. Each will set you a problem to solve. If you reach the

As you enter the land of the quest, a small figure approaches and you realize it is a foot soldier of the White King.

"You have a puzzle for me?" you ask.

"Of course, of course," says the foot soldier, and he leads you through the trees to a chess board set up with the position shown on the board below.

"White to play and mate in six," says the foot soldier.

"Mate in six?" you exclaim. "That is rather a lot of moves."

The foot soldier just laughs.

"Any Puzzle Master playing White would definitely mate in six moves," he says, and he runs away.

Can you find the right solution and advance one step along your journey?

end of the quest you will be able to call yourself a true Puzzle Master.

Do not worry if you cannot solve all the problems. You become a Puzzle Master not by finding all the answers, but through the knowledge you gain by working on the solutions. Good luck on your quest.

After working on the foot soldier's puzzle, you look around for a place to rest. All of a sudden you hear the sound of snorting and thundering hooves. You look up and see a mighty Knight on horseback.

"Foot soldiers only know silly puzzles," says the Knight disdainfully. "I will show you a real chess problem."

He leads you over a bridge to another chess board set up with the position shown above.

"Now this is a real puzzle," says the Knight proudly. "White, to play, achieves help-mate in four moves."

"You mean that White moves first, and that White and Black then move in such a way that Black mates White on the fourth move?"

"Precisely," says the Knight and rides off, leaving you with the second puzzle on your quest.

Can you see how Black, with White's help, is able to deliver mate in four moves?

Now you are well on your way along the quest and there is no turning back. You walk along the dusty path, wondering what your next problem will be, when you hear a soft, rather shy voice addressing you from behind. You turn around and see a Bishop, dressed in splendid robes and smiling at you gently.

"Knights are so terribly rude," says the Bishop, "and their problems are always so confusing, don't you find?"

"Well," you say, not quite sure what answer is expected of you.

"Have a look at this," says the Bishop, leading you through some gates to a chess board with the position shown below.

"Isn't this a beautiful problem?" says the Bishop. "White, to play, has to mate Black in two moves. Very straightforward really, unlike the previous problem."

"Well, it's not that simple," you object. "After all, there are rather too many Bishops."

"There are never too many Bishops," snaps your companion in an offended tone.

Can you see the mate in two for White? (To set up the position on your chess board, use Pawns for the Bishops.)

You set off again along the path. As you turn a corner, you are confronted by a majestic castle towering before you. You sigh with awe and your wonder grows as you hear a voice from behind the battlements.

"The Rook is a stately piece and it is now time for a majestic puzzle," booms the voice.

The next moment the drawbridge is lowered and two soldiers dash out. They arrange the position shown on the board above and quickly retreat.

A moment later you hear the resounding voice again.

"In this position, White, to play, is able to mate Black in three moves. But that is not all. White has a choice of three different first moves, all of which lead to mate in three. Think hard and try to find all three solutions."

With that, the drawbridge is raised and you are left alone with your task: to find three different three-move mates for White. Can you discover all three mates?

Your quest is going well but you now have to face the Queen, who is renowned for her perverse and dominating ways. Indeed, your heart sinks as she strides purposefully towards you and presents you with an empty chess board.

"Your task," says the Queen, "is to take eight Queens of the same colour and place them on the chess board in such a way that none of them controls a square that is occupied by another."

"You mean I have to put each of the Queens on a square that is not attacked by the seven other Queens?"

"Precisely," says the Queen. "I should warn you that there is no unique solution. There are many ways in which you may solve the task, but you need find only one of them." (For the eight Queens, use the Pawns from your chess set.)

You are almost there! In the distance you can see the King approaching, smiling confidently, a crown on his head and a sceptre in his hand. With great dignity, the King sets up the position shown below and together you study the arrangement of the pieces on the board.

"An interesting position, don't you think?" says the King.

"Yes, certainly," you reply, not quite sure what to make of it.

"And you notice, of course, that Black has no King?"

"Yes, clearly, Black has no King," you nod.

"Very well," says the King. "You must place the Black King on the board, so that White, to play, is able to deliver mate in three moves."

The King turns and strides off across the lawns and you are left with the final puzzle in your Master Quest.

Puzzle Master

Clues

Page 6　Bishop puzzles

4. Which pieces are exposed when the Black King moves out of check?

Page 7　Rook puzzles

2. To catch the Knight, try attacking the King.

4. Note that the Pawn on a3 is pinned to the King so it cannot guard square b4.

Page 9　King puzzles

3. What has White not yet done on this board?

Pages 10-11　Checkmate in one

2. The mating net around the Black King is nearly complete. Which White piece can move in to deliver mate?

3. Black's mate is quite simple, but for White, remember, it is sometimes best to underpromote a Pawn.

5. Which White piece can take a piece and check the King – without being taken itself?

7. Sometimes it is best to promote a Pawn to a piece other than a Queen.

8. White should have played **1.e4** to give the White King an escape square.

Pages 12-13　Two-move mates

2. Note that the h7 Pawn cannot move as it is defending the King from attack by the h1 Rook.

3. On this board there is no need to put the King in check on the first move.

5. Try using the White g-Pawn to help trap the enemy King.

7. White has lost control of the h1–a8 diagonal because the *fianchettoed* Bishop has been captured. This leaves the g2 square rather vulnerable.

8. White's King is well placed and the Pawns on f2 and g2 cover the Black King's escape squares. Can you spot a move for the White Knight that will ensure checkmate on the following move?

Pages 14-15　More two-movers

1. Black to move. Look for a powerful Black sacrifice that removes the Pawn on g2 and allows the b1 Bishop to mate the White King from square e4.

2. Black to move. The Black Bishop on d5 has a powerful mating threat. Can you spot it?

3. Black to move. White cannot force mate in two, but Black has a powerful Queen move.

4. This is a tricky one. It could be Black, but then again, it might be White.

First you need to study the position of each King and try to decide which side is in a position to deliver mate. Black's King is vulnerable because it is almost surrounded by Pawns – the only move for the King is **1...Kxe4**. Can White block this move and so trap the King and then deliver mate?

On the other hand, White's King is also in an awkward position. The only move for the King is **1.Kxe8**, which would expose it to a Rook check from h8. White's only other move is **1.d3**. If Black could block this move, Black might be able to mate the White King. So who is winning – Black or White?

5. Black has two strong Knight moves and, since White is threatening mate, Black must start with a check.

Pages 16-17　Tactics and combinations

1. Black's King and Rooks are vulnerable as they are all on black squares and can be attacked by White's black-squared Bishop. Also, the Black King and d6 Rook can be forked by the e5 Pawn. Can you see how White can sacrifice a Pawn to win an important Black piece with a skewer?

2. Although Black's Queen is pinned to the King, it can still move as long as it does not expose the King. Note also that three of White's pieces – the King, Queen and Bishop – are vulnerable to a skewer attack.

3. If Black moves the Knight on f6, the Black Queen can move down from the back rank to attack.

4. Imagine there were no White Pawn on f2. The Black Queen could then move to h4 and deliver mate. Can you think of a useful Knight move which would enable you to put this idea into practice?

5. Note that the Black King and Queen are on the same diagonal and open to fork attacks.

6. One way to protect the Pawn so it can reach the Queening square is to block the e-file. Can you see how Black can sacrifice a piece to block the file so the Pawn is protected from the Rook's firepower?

7. White cannot stop the threat to the Pawn from the Black Rook but it may be to White's advantage for Black to take this Pawn, for then the Black Rook and King will be on the same rank…

Pages 18-19   Sacrifice to win

3. White's best attacking piece is the Queen, but it is pinned to the King. Which piece can White sacrifice to free the Queen?

5. At present the King has two escape squares – d2 and d4. Can you find a way to bring the King out and trap it in a mating net?

6. The White Knight is blocking the Rook's line of attack. Can you find a move for the Knight that will weaken Black's defences and open the lines for the White Rook?

8. At first glance, the Black King seems well defended by Pawns. But the f7 Pawn is pinned by the White Bishop on b3, the h7 Pawn is blocking the h-file so the White Rook cannot deliver mate, and the g6 Pawn is attacked by the mighty Queen on b1.

Pages 20-21   Study puzzles

1. How can White make the two Bishops work together to complete the mating net around the King? It is important to control escape squares g7 and h8.

2. To deliver mate, not only does White need to leave the a2 Rook where it is, but White also has to move the c8 Rook to a square that is controlled by Black. This is an example of how a study may involve unusual moves.

3. Can you find a way for the b3 Bishop to attack square d7 and complete the mating net around the King?

5. In this puzzle, giving check will not help. You need to move the Queen to increase her firepower. Hint: Try moving back to where you started.

6. Again, a Queen move is required, but this time you must give a check. Do not play **1.Qd3**, though – that was the mistake Norwood made!

Pages 22-23   Save yourself puzzles

1. You have to sacrifice the Queen and then find a way to give perpetual check with the Knight.

2a). Only one of the White pieces can move. With this piece, White can force a draw using either perpetual check or stalemate.

3. Of the two ways to draw, perpetual check and stalemate, perpetual check is clearly impossible as Black has no pieces with which to check the enemy King.

For stalemate, Black must have no legal moves, in other words, both the Black King and the h-Pawn must be blocked. To achieve this, you need to find a way for Black to trap the King with the h-Pawn and the h-Pawn with the King.

Pages 24-25   Advanced winning techniques

1. The first thing to notice on this board is that Black is threatening to win at once with **1...Qxg2++**. There is nothing White can do against this mating threat: **1.g3**, **Qg2++**; or **1.Kf1**, **Qxf2++**; or **1.Bf1**, **Rxg2+**; **2.Bxg2**, **Qxg2++**; or even **1.Be4**, **Rxg2+**; **2.Kh1**, **Rg4+** discovered check from the Queen on f3; **3.Bxf3**, **Bxf3++**.

Since you know that Black can deliver mate, you must make sure Black is kept busy elsewhere by keeping Black in check. Now you know that every single one of White's moves must put Black in check, you should be able to see the start of the combination.

Clues continued over the page.   **41**

Pages 24-25 continued

3. If it were Black's move next, Black would be in stalemate and the game would be a draw. So first you must give Black the chance to move. You can play **1.d6**, or move the White King, but after **1.d6**, the quickest mate is **1...exd6**; **2.Kf7**, **d5**; **3.e5**, **d4**; **4.e6**, **d3**; **5.e7++**. Since your task is to mate in four, not five, you must concentrate on your King.

To which square should the King move? If you choose f7 or f5, then Black's reply **1...e5** stops White's attack momentarily as **2.dxe6** en passant is stalemate. The only square for White's King is e5. Now Black can play **1...e6** and White must think again as **2.Kxe6** is stalemate and **2.dxe6** allows the Black King to escape from the back rank with **2...Ke7**.

So White must try something different, such as advancing the d-Pawn, which leaves Black with only one move, **2...cxd6+**. To plan your combination, remember that it is best if each of your moves leaves Black with only one possible reply.

6. You might be tempted to move the Knight on g3 to bring about a discovered check from the Queen, but this would not get you very far. Instead, you should look for ways to make the Black pieces work together. The Rook on b3, for example, is out of play, since it is blocked by the Bishop on e3. In the same way, the Queen on e5 would be threatening to take the Rook on e1 if the Bishop were not blocking its path. So, it is the Bishop that you should move as it hinders your other forces.

Pages 26-27 Help-mate puzzles

3. The Black Knight cannot cover enough squares to mate the enemy King, but as this is a help-mate puzzle, try using the White Rook to help trap its own King.

5. The White King cannot be mated in the middle of the board, so you need to find a mating position, for example, the corner where it is most vulnerable. Also, you can only deliver mate with a King and a Bishop if the enemy King is trapped by one of its own pieces, so the White Bishop will have to block one of its own King's escape squares.

6. One of the most common mates is the back rank mate. For Black to deliver a back rank mate within three moves, you need to cover escape squares f2 and h2 with White pieces and remove the Rooks on d1 and e1.

Pages 28-29 Retro-puzzles

2. Here are some of the conclusions Mrs Black arrived at from studying the board:

a) Black's h7 Pawn has captured a piece on g6 and it is the only Black Pawn to have moved.
b) White's h-Pawn may have moved, and it has definitely disappeared. None of the other White Pawns has moved.
c) The White piece taken on g6 cannot have been the h-Pawn. In order to get on to the g-file the White Pawn would have had to have made a capture and Black has not lost any pieces.
d) The only White pieces that could have reached g6 are the h1 Rook and the b1 and g1 Knights, but White is a Pawn down – not a Rook or a Knight. So, and this was Mrs Black's real breakthrough, White must have promoted the h-Pawn to a Rook or Knight.

One last hint – the Rook on h1 need not be the one that started the game on that square. Remember, in retro-puzzles, things are not always as they seem.

Pages 30-31 Brainteasers

1. When you place the Kings on the board there is no reason why the White King should not be in check. It could even be placed right next to the Queen for instance...

3. In fact, every single White move puts Black in check, but for just one of the moves, Black can defend against the check. Can you find a move for White that unpins the Black Rook on b7 so Black can defend the King?

4. It seems impossible for the g1 and g8 Knights to have captured each other in just four moves, and the catch is – they did not! This is a retro-puzzle and in retro-puzzles you should not be taken in by appearances. Can you be sure that the Black Knight on b8 is the one that started the game on that square?

Pages 32-33 Mate the Grandmaster

2. White's position is not as hopeless as it looks. First, to avoid instant defeat, White must give check with the Rook. The Black King moves to apparent safety on h7. Now you need to keep the King in check, perhaps by making a sacrifice, and to use the strength of the Bishop along the a1–h8 diagonal to support one of your most powerful pieces.

3. Black must keep White in check so that White has no chance to deliver mate. It would be worth a grand sacrifice to achieve this objective.

6. The Pawn on g2 is pinned to the White King. It would be worth the greatest sacrifice to tempt the Black Rook away from this pin.

Page 35 Puzzle Master Quest

Remember that this is a help-mate puzzle and the easiest place to checkmate the King is in the corner. A King and Knight cannot mate a lone King, so you need to use the White Knight to help form a mating net by placing it next to its own King. Now you know where the White pieces are placed, you should be able to deduce the mating positions for the Black pieces. A further clue is that each piece has to move twice.

Quest page 36

The Bishop has set a difficult puzzle. At first sight the position seems symmetrical, but when there are Pawns on the board, such symmetry is a decoy, as Pawns can only move forwards. This should tell you which end of the board to study. Also, since the two Bishops on the right are at the edge of the board, they are not as powerful as the Bishops on d2 and d6. This is a clue to which side of the board you should work on.

Now try thinking about Black's responses to White's first move. Whichever piece White moves, Black can move only the Pawn on e3 or g3. See if you can follow this idea through, remembering that Bishops have more firepower on open lines away from the edge of the board.

Quest page 37

In most puzzles where the King and Rook are on their starting squares, the solution involves castling. In this puzzle, however, none of the solutions involve castling.

The neatest solution involves a sacrifice to lure the King to the side of the board where it will be easier to deliver mate. It should not be too difficult to spot which Rook to sacrifice. You then need to bring the White King forward to force the Black King into the mating net.

To help you find the other solutions, note that White, to play, can capture the Pawn with either Rook. Two further clues are that Black is mated on either e3 or g1, and the White King does not move.

Like the Bishop's puzzle, this position appears symmetrical, this time along the e1–h4 diagonal. In fact, the solutions, depending on which Rook takes the Pawn, are reflections of each other. If you work out the solution for one Rook, then hold a mirror near the board, parallel to the e1–h4 diagonal, you should spot how the King is mated when the other Rook takes the Pawn.

Quest page 38

There are many possible solutions to this problem, so you are not looking for one particular position. To approach the solution logically, however, think about how the Queen moves. It can move in the same way as every piece on the board except the Knight. The best way to place the Queens so they do not control the same squares, is Knight-moves away from each other.

Quest page 39

The best place to mate the King is in a corner, or near an edge of the board. Since all the White pieces are still on their starting squares, however, a corner would be too far away for a mate in three. So this should give you a general idea of where the King is placed.

Next, you need to decide whether it is easier to mate on the Kingside or the Queenside. White's first move, which is **1.d4**, should give you a clue.

Answers

Page 4 Pawn puzzles

1. Black can play **1...e1**, promote the Pawn to a Queen or Rook, and checkmate the White King, which is trapped by its own Pawns.

2. **1.fxe5+** captures the Knight – a more valuable piece than the Pawn on g5.

3. **1.gxh3** is the best move because the Black Pawn on h3 is close to promoting.

4. White can play **1.h6**. When Black replies **1...gxh6**, the g-rank is open and the g-Pawn can advance to the promoting square.

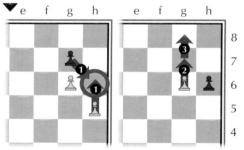

DID YOU KNOW?

● Many Grandmasters have extraordinary powers of memory. For example, the great American player, Bobby Fischer, is said never to have forgotten a single game he played or saw.

● Top players sometimes demonstrate their skills by performing exhibitions, where they take on several opponents at once. To make their task more difficult, they may wear blindfolds so that they have to keep track in their heads of all the positions. One player, Janos Flesch, managed to play an amazing 52 blindfold games at once.

Page 5 Knight puzzles

1. **1.Nxf6+** is the best move since it takes the Rook – a valuable piece.

2. **1.Nxg4+**. This move wins a Pawn and forks the King and Rook. The Black King has to move out of check, so the Knight can take the Rook next move.

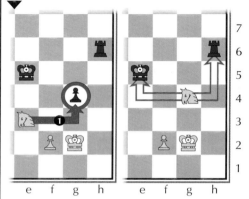

3. **1.Nb6+**. When a Knight checks the enemy King, the opponent has to move the King or capture the Knight. The Knight can hop over pieces, so the King cannot be defended by moving a piece between the Knight and King.

Here, the King is blocked in by a Pawn and the Queen, and White's Bishop is attacking b8. Black's only option is to play **1...Qxb6**. White can then take the Queen with **2.cxb6**.

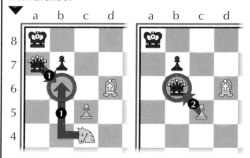

4. Both **1...Nb3** and **1...Nc2** are mate. Note how, by moving the Knight, Black unleashes the power of the Bishop. White is in double check and mate.

Page 6 Bishop puzzles

1. **1.Bb2++**. To checkmate with a King and two Bishops against a King, you need to trap the King in the corner.

2. Black should play **1...Bc8**, so the Bishop covers the critical a6–c8 diagonal and stops any of White's Pawns from advancing.

3. **1...Be2+** forks the King and Knight. When the King moves, Black can take the Knight. This is better than **1...Bxh5**, winning only the h-Pawn.

▼

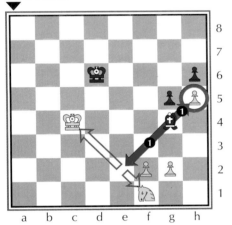

4. **1.Bh3+** is the best move as it skewers the Black Queen. When the King moves, the Queen will be captured. **1.Bd3+** would skewer the Rook – a less valuable piece.

▼

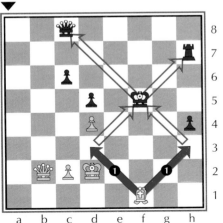

Page 7 Rook puzzles

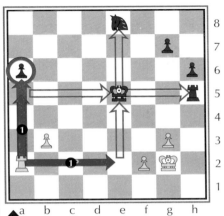

1. The best move is **1.Ra5+**, which will capture the Rook on h5 after the King moves. **1.Rxa6** wins only a Pawn and **1.Re2+** captures the e8 Knight with a skewer attack.

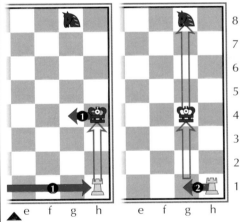

2. **1.Rh1+** forces the Black King on to the g-file so that, after **2.Rg1+**, the Rook will win the Knight on g8 with a skewer attack.

3. **1...Rh1++**.

4. Black can play **1...Rb4+**, forking the King and Knight and taking the Knight next turn. The a3 Pawn cannot take the Rook as it is pinned to the King by the Rook on a1. Nor can the White King take the Rook as the b4 square is attacked by the Pawn on c5.

Page 8   Queen puzzles

1. **1.Qg7++**. Note that if White plays **1.Qa8+**, Black blocks with **1...Bf8** and the game continues.

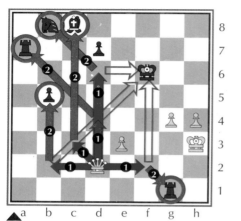

2. The Queen has the five checking moves shown on the board above. **1.Qf2+** wins the Rook on g1. **1.Qd4+** wins the Rook on a7. **1.Qd6+** wins the Knight on b8 and **1.Qc3+** wins the Bishop on c8. **1.Qb2+** wins the Pawn on b5. Such is the power of the Queen.

3. Avoid the disastrous **1.Qh1+**, followed by **2.Qxb7**, capturing the Rook when the King moves. Black can play **2...Nc5+**, forking the White King and Queen, as shown below. Safer is **1.Qe5+** (shown at the bottom) or **1.Qe1+, Kd5; 2.Qe5+**, winning the Knight on e6 with a fork attack.

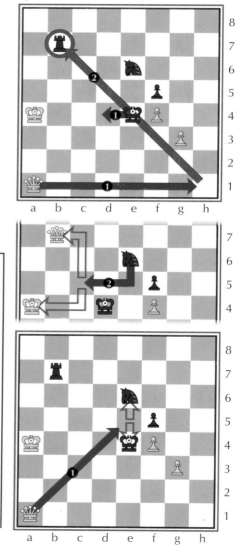

4. **1...Qb8++**. Note that the advancing Pawns are unable to help. The Pawn on a7 cannot take the Queen as it is pinned by the a1 Rook.

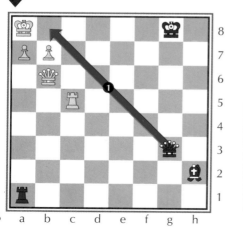

Page 9 King puzzles

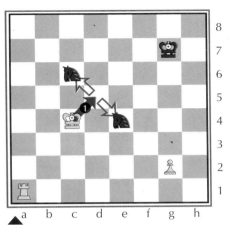

1. **1.Kd5** forks the two Knights. This is an unusual role reversal that wins White a Knight. Usually it is the Knight which carries out a fork.

2. **1...Kc7++**. The White King is trapped in the corner and mated by a discovered check from the Bishop.

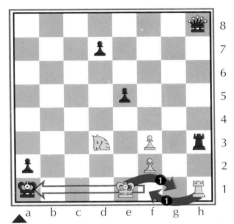

3. White's mating move is **1.0-0++**. In this example, White was wise not to castle too early in the game.

4. **1.Kf4** is the way to *zugzwang* Black, that is, put Black in a position where every move will lead to disaster. Black's only move is **1...g3**. White can then play **2.hxg3++**.

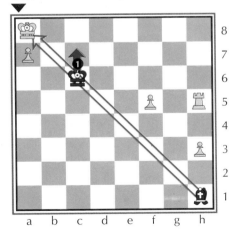

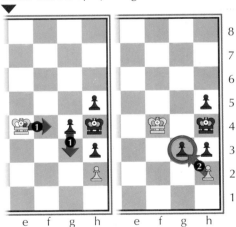

DID YOU KNOW? The great American player Harry Pilsbury had an amazing memory. He was able to play up to 22 games at once while wearing a blindfold, and at the same time, take part in a game of whist. What's more, he would memorize a long list of words given to him by the spectators at the beginning of the display, and repeat it perfectly at the end.

Pages 10-11 Checkmate in one

1. The winning move is **1.Bf6++**. In the actual game, Grandmaster Svetozar Gligorić of Yugoslavia played **1.Rd1+** and just managed to win after 19 more moves.

2. The Grandmaster played **1.Re5++**, as shown in the diagram on the right. ▶

3. Black can play **1...Rh6++**. White can mate with **1.dxc8(N)++**, underpromoting the Pawn to a Knight.

4. **1.Bd8++**. This stops the King escaping to b6. When looking for checkmate, always remember to cut off every one of the King's escape squares.

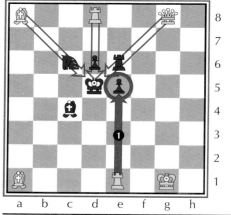

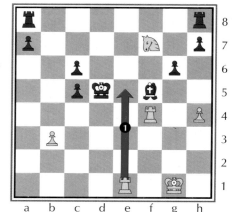

◀ 5. **1.Rxe5++**. None of Black's pieces can take the Rook – they are all pinned to the King, as shown in the diagram on the left.

6. **1...Bd3++**, double check and mate from the Bishop and Rook. If, instead, the Bishop moved to h3, the King could still escape to e2. ▼

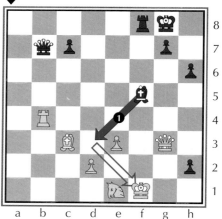

◀ 7. White can play **1.f8(N)++**, underpromoting to a Knight as shown in the two pictures on the left. This mates the King by enabling the h7 Rook to defend the e7 Pawn, and allowing the Bishop on h5 to cover square e8.

8. Black played **1...Nd3++**. The Pawn on e2 is pinned by the Black Queen so the White King is trapped in a smothered mate.

Pages 12-13   Two-move mates

1. **1...Nh3+** forces White to play **2.Kh1**. Black can then play **2...Bb7++**. To mate with a King, Bishop and Knight against a lone King, you need to force the enemy King on to a corner square of the same colour as the diagonals along which your Bishop can move.

2. After **1.Ne7+**, Black can play only **1...Kh8**. Now White can play **2.Nfxg6++** (shown on the right). Did you see that Black's Pawn on h7 cannot take the Knight as it is pinned to the King by the White Rook on h1?

3. **1.Rh1** is the winning move. White is not checking the enemy King but there is no way Black can avoid White's next move: **2.Kg1++**.

4. Black can play **1...Nf3+**, shielding the King from check and at the same time, checking White so that White's next move, **2.Kh1** is forced. Black can now play **2...Rxh2++**. Note that White's Queen is pinned by the Rook on a1 and cannot capture the Knight.

5. White can win with **1.g5+**. If Black takes the Pawn with **1...Kxg5**, then White can play **2.Qf4++** (see right). Alternatively, if Black plays **1...Bxg5**, then White can play **2.Qg7++** or **2.Rh8++** (far right). In the actual game, Grandmaster Samuel Reshevsky played **1.Qxg6+** and lost his Queen.

6. The only way to mate is **1.Rg8+**, and discovered check from the c3 Bishop. The Black King now has to take the Rook with **1...Kxg8** and White wins with **2.Rg1++**.

7. If Black plays **1...Bh3**, White, having no Bishop to control the squares around the King, cannot prevent **2...Qg2++**. Making the Queen and Bishop work together like this is one of the most common ways of mating the enemy King, especially when your opponent has no Bishop to control the diagonal.

8. White can win with **1.Ng1**. White now has two mating threats: **2.g3+** and **2.Nf3+** (shown on the right). Black can only tackle one threat at a time. If Black plays **1...Bc7** to stop White from playing **2.g3**, then White wins with **2.Nf3++**. If Black plays **1...g4** to prevent **2.Nf3**, then White wins with **2.g3++**.

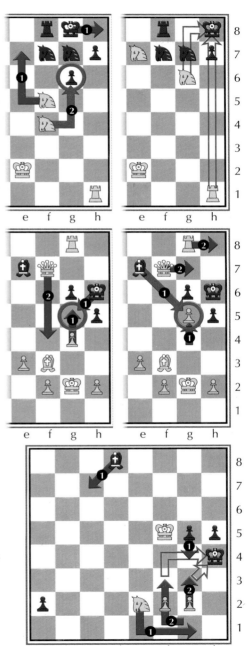

Pages 14-15   More two-movers

1. Black can win by sacrificing the Rook with
1...Rxh3+; 2.gxh3, Be4++ as shown on the
right.

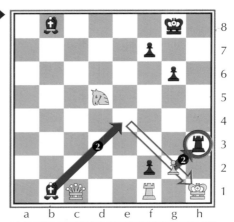

2. It is in fact Black who can force mate. After
1...f6, Black threatens **2...Bf7++**. If White
plays **2.g5** to give the King an escape square,
then Black wins with **2...Bf3++**.

3. Again, it is Black who can mate in two.
After **1...Qf1**, whatever White plays, Black
will reply with **2...Qg2++**.

4. The winning move is **d3** and the trick is
that either side can win with this move. If
White plays first (**1.d3**), Black cannot prevent
White playing **2.Bf4++**, as shown below.
▼ *Solution continued below right.*

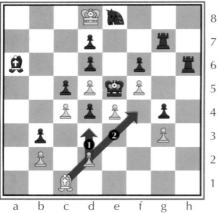

If Black plays **1...d3** (shown above), White's
only move is **2.Kxe8**, as all the White Pawns
are blocked. Black now wins with **2...Rh8++**.

◀ 5. Black can win with **1...Nf3+** or **1...Nh3+**
(shown left). After **1...Nf3+**, White is forced to
play **2.Kh1** and is mated by **2...Qxh2++**. If
Black plays **1...Nh3+**, White again has to play
2.Kh1 and Black wins with **2...Bxg2++**.

6. White can play **1.Ba7+**, forcing Black to
move **1...Ka8**. White can then play **2.Qc8++**.
   Alternatively, White can win by sacrificing
the Rook as follows: **1.Ra8+, Kxa8; 2.Qc8++**.
Both methods win by forcing the King into the
corner so the Queen can attack in safety.

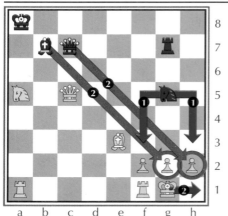

Pages 16-17   Tactics and combinations

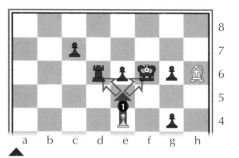

1. **1.e5+** forks the King and d6 Rook (shown above). Black can either move the King and lose the Rook, or play **1...Kxe5**. White can then skewer the King and a1 Rook with **2.Bg7+**, winning the Rook when the King moves (shown right). If White skewered the d6 Rook with **2.Bf4**, followed by **3.Bxd6**, then Black could take the Bishop with the c7 Pawn.

2. Black can play the crushing combination **1...Qxb4+; 2.Kxb4, Ra4+**. After White's King moves away, Black takes the Queen on g4.

3. Black can play **1...Nxe4**. After White recaptures with either **2.fxe4** or **2.Nxe4**, Black can play **2...Qh4+**, checking the White King and forking the White Bishop on h6, which can be taken next move.

4. Black can play **1...Ne3**. White's Queen is attacked and cannot move away. If White takes the Knight with **2.fxe3**, then Black can win the game with **2...Qh4+; 3.g3, Qxg3++**.

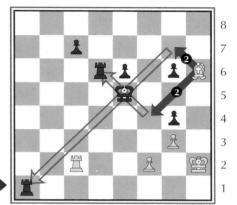

5. White should play **1.Bc5+**, sacrificing the Bishop in a fork attack on the Black King and Queen. After **1...Qxc5**, White can play **2.Ne6+**, this time forking the King and Queen with the Knight, and taking the Queen next move after the King has moved away.

6. Black's winning move is **1...Be6+**, forking the King and Rook. White is forced to play **2.Kxe6** and now the White King shields Black's Pawn from attack by the Rook, and Black can promote the Pawn.

7. White should play **1.Rh8**, threatening to promote the a-Pawn. If Black replies with **1...Rxa7**, White can play **2.Rh7+**, a skewer attack on the King and Rook that wins the Rook next turn.

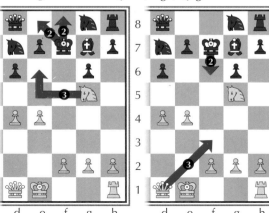

8. White's best move would have been **1.Bxf7+**. If Black plays **1...Kf8**, he remains a Pawn down and if he plays **1...Kxf7**, he has to put up with **2.Ng5+**. After this Knight check, Black can make three different moves, all of which are disastrous for Black, as shown in the diagrams on the left.
   If Black plays **2...Kf8** or **2...Ke8**, as shown far left, then **3.Ne6** wins the Queen on d8 (the pieces are shown after White's second move). Alternatively, if Black decides to try **2...Kf6**, as shown on the left, then White wins the game with **3.Qf3++**.

51

Pages 18-19   Sacrifice to win

1. White can play **1.Qg7+**, sacrificing the Queen to the Knight when Black replies with **1…Nxg7**. Now the Black King is trapped in a cage of its own pieces and White can use the Knight to hop in and deliver smothered mate with **2.Nf6++**.

DID YOU KNOW? Smothered mate, where the King is trapped by its own pieces and mated by a Knight, has been a popular winning position since the eighteenth century.

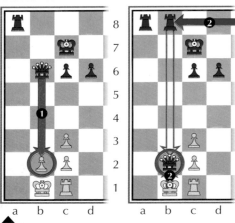

7. White should sacrifice the Queen with **1.Qg8+**. After **1…Rxg8**, White wins with **2.Nf7++**.

8. Again, White should sacrifice the Queen. After **1.Qxg6+**, Black cannot move the King, nor can the Queen be taken by the f-Pawn as it is pinned by the Bishop on b3, as shown below. Black has no choice but **1…hxg6**, after which White wins with **2.Rh8++**.

2. Black can win by sacrificing the Queen: **1…Qxb2+; 2.Kxb2, Rgb8++**, as shown in the diagrams above. When the enemy King is defended by only a thin line of Pawns, the attacking side should try to break it up. Often the only way to do this is with a sacrifice.

3. To release the Queen from the Rook pin, White should play **1.Rd8+**. Black has to take the Rook with **1…Rxd8**. White can then deal the final blow with **2.Qxa7++**.

4. Norwood played **1.Rxa7+**. Black had to take the Rook with **1…Kxa7**, and White could then mate with **2.Qa5++**. Did you notice that the Black Queen is pinned to the King by the White Queen and so cannot take the Rook?

5. The only way for Black to achieve checkmate is **1…Bb4+; 2.Kxb4, Qa5++**. As in Puzzle 1, sacrificing a piece helps to trap the enemy King in a cage of its own pieces.

6. White is lucky to have the forcing combination **1.Nb6+**, to which Black has to reply **1…axb6** so White can win with **2.Ra4++**.

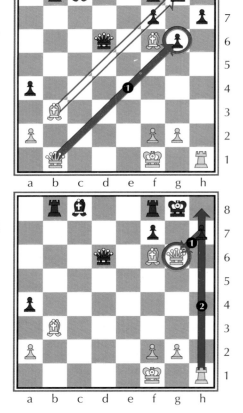

Pages 20-21 Study puzzles

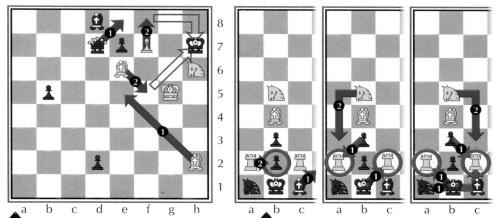

1. To give mate, White can play **1.Be5**. This leaves the Black King trapped, since White threatens checkmate by underpromoting the Pawn on f8 to a Knight with **2.f8(N)++** (see above). The only defence is **1...Qe8**, but then **2.Bf5++** is an alternative mate.

2. **1.Rc2** will mate Black next move. If Black moves the c1 Bishop, then White mates with **2.Raxb2++** (above left). If Black plays **1...Kxc2** or **1...bxa2**, White mates with **2.Na3++** (centre). If Black plays **1...Kxa2**, **1...Nxc2**, or **1...bxc2**, White mates with **2.Nc3++** (right).

3. White's move is **1.Ba4.** It may seem crazy to move the Bishop from the same diagonal as the Black King, but an unusual move like this is often the key to the study. From a4, the Bishop covers square d7 and completes the mating net around the Black King, shown on the right. If Black captures the Knight that is now unprotected on d5, then the Bishop returns to b3 to give mate. If Black plays **1...d6**, White wins with **2.Nbc7++**. Other possibilities are **1...e4**; **2.Qxe4++**, or **1...f5**; **2.Qg8++**, or **1...f6**; **2.Ndc7++**.

4. **1.Kg8** completes the mating net around the Black King, so mate is inevitable: **1...Qxg5+**; **2.Bg7++** discovered check and mate from the Queen on b6, for example, or **1...Rxf6**; **2.Qxf6++**. Or, if Black plays **1...Qb1** (to stop **2.Rh7++**), then White plays **2.Nf7++**.

5. **1.Qd1** leaves Black in *zugzwang.* If Black plays **1...Kd3**, then **2.Rxd5++**. If **1...Kc5**, **2.Qg1** is mate since the d5 Pawn is pinned to the King by the Rook on e5 and is not able to block the check. Capturing the Rook with **1...Kxe5** provokes **2.d4++**.

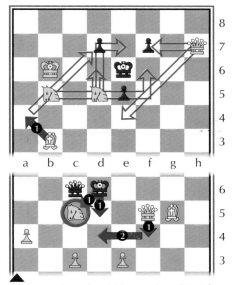

6. Our author should have played **1.Qf4+**. The Black King can then capture the Knight on c5 or move to d5, as shown above. Either way, **2.Qd4++** leaves Black in checkmate.

53

Pages 22-23   Save yourself puzzles

1. White draws by sacrificing the Queen and then causing perpetual check: **1.Qxf8+**, **Nxf8**; **2.Nf7+**, **Kg8** (see below left); **3.Nh6+**, **Kh8**; **4.Nf7+** and so on, as shown below right. The Black King is trapped on squares g8 and h8 and cannot escape from check as the White Knight hops between f7 and h6.

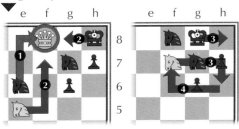

2a) The only piece White can move is the Rook. The Pawns are blocked and the White King cannot move. If White plays **1.Rg8+** and Black takes the Rook with **1...Kxg8**, the game ends in stalemate as White has no other pieces that can move.

If, however, the Black King tries to escape from the White Rook, the game ends in a draw as follows: **1...Kh7**; **2.Rg7+**, **Kh6**; **3.Rh6+**, **Kh5**; **4.Rg5+**, **Kh4** (**4...Bxg5** is stalemate); **5.Rh4+** perpetual check.

b) Without the Pawn on e5, the Black Queen can defend square g7 and White will lose as shown below: **1.Rg8+**, **Kh7**; **2.Rg7+**, **Qxg7**; **3.Kc1** (White's only move), **Qb2++**.

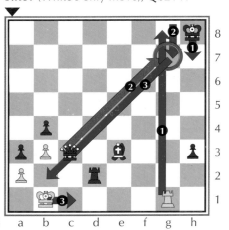

3. Black has an ingenious series of moves that leads to stalemate: **1...Kg6** (or **Kh6** – it makes no difference); **2.a5**, **Kh5**; **3.a6**, **Kh4**; **4.a7**, **h5**; **5.a8(Q)** and Black has no legal moves left. Note that there is nothing White can do about Black's manoeuvre.

4. White can either win or force a draw, whichever piece Black chooses for the Pawn.

a) Pawn to Knight – White wins with **2.Qd1++**.

b) Pawn to Bishop – White can again win with **2.Qd1++**.

c) Pawn to Rook – White can force a draw with **2.Qb5+**, **Qxb5** and the game ends in stalemate as White has no legal move.

d) Pawn to Queen – White can force a draw with **2.Qd1+**, **Qxd1**, again ending the game in stalemate with no legal move for White. Note that **2.Qb5+** does not work because Black is not compelled to capture the Queen and can play a move such as **2...Kc2**, leaving Black a Queen up and guaranteeing a win for Black.

DID YOU KNOW?   Napoleon was a keen but mediocre chess player. After making himself emperor, however, he rarely lost a game as hardly anyone dared to beat him.

Pages 24-25 Advanced winning techniques*

1. The winning combination is **1.Qxd7+**, **Kxd7**; **2.Bf5+** (double check from the Rook and Bishop), **Ke8**; **3.Bd7+**, **Kf8**; **4.Bxe7++** (or **2...Kc6**; **3.Bd7++**). Note how White uses some common attacking ideas, first sacrificing the Queen to draw out the King and put Black in check, then playing double check, which forces Black's King to move so White can play two powerful Bishop checks and deliver mate.

2. If White plays **1.Qh6**, Black has no escape. White threatens to play **2.Qxg7++** and if Black tries to defend with **1...Bxh6**, White can reply with **2.Ne7++**. If, on the other hand, Black takes the Bishop with **1...Bxf6**, then White wins with **2.Nxf6+**, **Qxf6** (or **2...Kh8**; **3.Qxh7++**); **3.exf6** and whatever Black replies, White can play **4.Qg7++**.

3. White's winning combination is ingenious – every single move White plays leaves Black with only one possible reply: **1.Ke5**, **e6**; **2.d6**, **cxd6**; **3.Kxd6**, **e5**; **4.c7++**. Although White's main problem is to avoid stalemating Black, the fact that Black has so few replies means that White can control Black's moves.

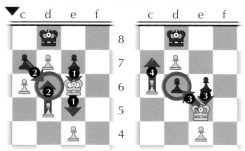

4. The winning combination is **1.Rg4+**, **fxg4**; **2.Qg5+**, **Kh8**; **3.Qh6**, and now Black is lost for moves. If Black tries to defend the Rook on f8 with **3...Qd8** or **3...Raa8**, then White wins with **4.Qxh7++**. If Black tries to avoid the mate on h7 with **3...f5** or **3...Bxd3**, then White wins with **4.Qxf8++**. Note how the sacrifice of the White Rook on g4 unleashes the Bishop's power by opening up the b1–h7 diagonal, and how the White Queen moves from f6 to g5 to h6 to bring about a double threat that wins on f8 or h7.

5. White can win with **1.Qxa7+**, **Kxa7** (reaching the position shown below left); **2.Ra2+**, **Qa4**; **3.Rxa4++**. White sacrifices the Queen to draw out the King. This leaves the King unprotected on the a-file, and cut off from the b-file by the White Rooks, as shown below right.

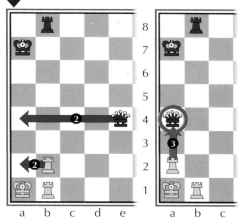

6. The winning move is **1...Bg1+**, a Bishop sacrifice. Now, White cannot avoid checkmate. If White takes the Bishop with the King (**2.Kxg1**), Black plays **2...Qxe1+**, followed by **3.Qf1**, **Qxf1+**; **4.Kh2**, **Qh1++**. Note how the sacrifice of the Bishop enables the Black Queen to take the Rook on e1 and allows the Knight on g3 to be protected by the Rook on b3.

If, on the other hand, White takes the Bishop with the Rook on g2 (**2.Rgxg1**), then Black mates as follows: **2...Nf1** double check – the discovered check from the Queen is now very strong as it is supported by the Knight check; **3.Kg2** (or **Kh1** – it makes no difference), **Qh2++**.

Alternatively, if White takes the Bishop with the Rook on e1 (**2.Rexg1**), then Black mates with **2...Nf1** double check; **3.Kh1**, **Rxh3+**; **4.Rh2**, **Rxh2++**.

Although the Bishop sacrifice looks a little surprising, it allows Black's other pieces to leap into action and it is only when they all work together that White can be mated.

* These answers are quite complicated, so it is a good idea to follow the moves on a chess board.

Answers continued

Pages 26-27 Help-mate puzzles

1. **1.Kd1** and Black mates with **1...Rh1++**.

2. White should move **1.Bg1** so Black can play **1...Kg3++** discovered check and mate.

3. **1.Kh1, Nf5; 2.Rh2, Ng3++**. The White King moves into the corner and is then trapped by the White Rook, while the Black Knight hops into battle position ready to deliver mate.

5. **1.Ke4, Kc6; 2.Kf3, Kd5; 3.Kg2, Ke4; 4.Kh1, Kf3; 5.Bh2, Kf2++**. The White King moves to h1, which is more vulnerable than a1 or h8 since it is on the diagonal occupied by the Black Bishop. The White Bishop then moves to h2 to trap the White King and the Black King moves to f2 to unleash the power of the Black Bishop, as shown in the diagram below.

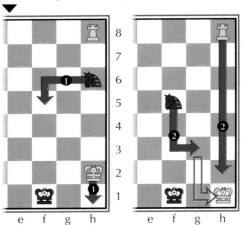

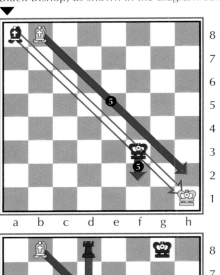

4. Help-mate is brought about with the following moves: **1...Ke7; 2.Kg7, Ke8; 3.Kf6, Kf8; 4.Rh8++**. The Black King stays on a vulnerable square at the edge of the board. The White King moves away from the edge of the board so it can attack more squares and make room for the Rook.

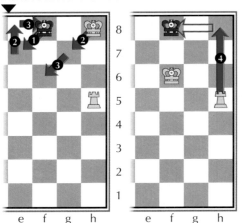

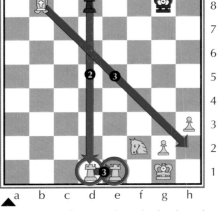

6. White can be mated on the back rank as follows: **1.Nf2, Rd8; 2.b8(B)** (reaching the position shown above), **Rxd1; 3.Bh2, Rxe1++**. The King is trapped by the White Knight and Bishop. Did you see that **2.b8(Q)** is not possible as it pins the Black Rook on d8?

Pages 28-29   Retro-puzzles

1. To find who could have taken the Black Knight, set up the position shown on the board and consider each piece in turn:

The Pawns – Obviously the Black Knight could not have been taken by a Pawn as the White e-Pawn has not moved diagonally for a capture, and none of the other White Pawns have moved at all.

The Knights – Knights can leap out from the back rank, so a White Knight could have taken the Black Knight and then returned to its position.

The King, Queen and captured Bishop – Since the White e-Pawn has advanced two squares, any one of these pieces could have marched out, captured the Knight and then returned to its place.

The Rooks – Even these could have captured the Knight. If both the White King and g-Knight moved, the h1 Rook would be free. Even the a1 Rook could have captured the Knight if, say, the White Knight on b1 had moved out and the Black Knight had moved down to b1 via c6, a5, c4 and a3. Afterwards, the Rook could have returned to a1 and the White Knight to b1. Unlikely, but possible.

The c1 Bishop – No, this piece could not have captured the Knight as it is imprisoned by the b2 and d2 Pawns.

So, the Black Knight could not have been captured by a White Pawn or by the Bishop on c1, but any of the other pieces might have taken it. Working on this kind of puzzle helps you to become aware of all the possible moves leading to even a simple position.

2. Mrs Black was right – the h1 Rook has moved and so White is not allowed to castle. The piece captured on g6 must have been a Knight or a Rook and not a Pawn, as the White Pawn could not reach the g-file without making a capture – and Black has not lost any pieces.

Since, however, White is a Pawn and not a Knight or a Rook down, White must have underpromoted the h-Pawn to a Knight or a Rook. White must have chosen to promote to a Rook, because a Knight would have been trapped on h8 as both f7 and g6 are occupied by Black Pawns.

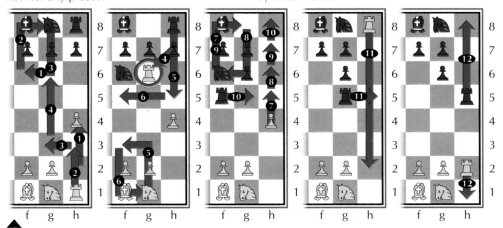

The moves made by the original players are listed here and shown on the five diagrams above: **1.h4**, **Nf6**; **2.Rh3**, **Ng8**; **3.Rg3**, **Nf6**; **4.Rg6** (diagram one), **hxg6**; **5.Nf3**, **Rh5**;

6.Ng1, **Rf5** (diagram two); **7.h5**, **Ng8**; **8.h6**, **Nf6**; **9.h7**, **Ng8**; **10.h8(R)**, **Rg5** (diagram three); **11.Rh2**, **Rh5** (diagram four); **12.Rh1**, **Rh8** (diagram five).

57

Pages 30-31 Brainteasers

1. The White King is on f3. The Black King is in the corner on h1, under fire from the two Bishops. White's mating move is **1.Kxf2++**, a discovered check from the Bishop on d5.

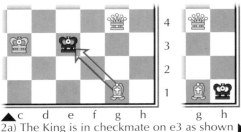

2a) The King is in checkmate on e3 as shown above left. b) The King is in stalemate on h1 (centre). c) The King is on a8 so that, after **1.Qc8**, Black is in checkmate (right).

3. White's move is **1.Rc6+**. On square c6, the White Rook blocks the h1–a8 diagonal and the Black Rook, which was pinned by the a8 Bishop, can now capture the Bishop on h7. This is the only solution to this puzzle – any other move would put Black in checkmate.

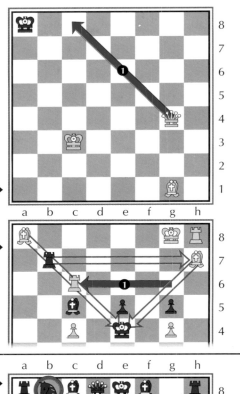

4. There are four ways to arrive at the position shown in the puzzle. For example: **1.Nf3**, **d5**; **2.Ne5**, **Nf6**; **3.Nc6** (shown above), **Nfd7**; **4.Nxb8**, **Nxb8** (shown in the two pictures right). It is the Black Knight on b8 which was captured and not the g8 Knight.

Another solution is: **1.Nf3**, **Nf6**; **2.Nd4**, **d5**; **3.Nc6**, **Nfd7**; **4.Nxb8**, **Nxb8**.

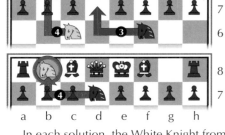

In each solution, the White Knight from g1 has to reach square c6 on its third move and this can be done via f3 and d4 or f3 and e5. The Black Knight on g8 has to reach square d7 on its third move. Black can do this by playing either **1...d5** or **1...Nf6**. As soon as the two Knights are on squares c6 and d7, the double Knight capture can take place.

Pages 32-33   Mate the Grandmaster

1. **1.Qg1+, Kd2; 2.Qc1+, Kd3; 3.Qc3++,**
giving the mating position shown below.

▼

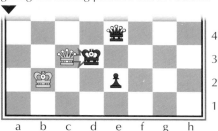

2. White can deliver mate in four as follows:
1.Rc8+, Kh7; 2.Rh8+, Kxh8 (giving the
position shown on the right); **3.Qh6+, Kg8**
(the g7 Pawn cannot capture the Queen as it
is pinned by the b2 Bishop, as shown in the
diagram); **4.Qxg7++.**

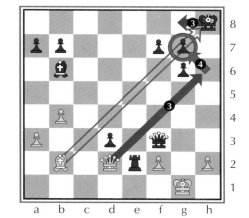

3. **1...Qg3+; 2.Kxg3.** Keres's sacrifice of
the Queen leaves White with no chance to
deliver mate. Now, when Keres promotes
the Pawn, the King is again in check and he
can deliver mate as shown in the two
diagrams on the right: **2...e1(Q)+; 3.Kh3,
Re3+; 4.Kh2, Qg3+; 5.Kg1, Re1++.** An
alternative mate is **3.Kh2, Qxh4+; 4.Kg1,
Re1++.**

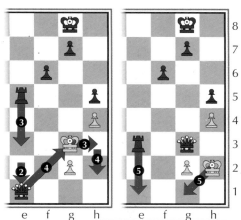

4. Ivkov's Pawn move opened the a1–h8
diagonal. White should play **1.Bc3** to
strenghthen White's control of the a1–h8
diagonal so Black is unable to prevent the
inevitable **2.Qh8++.**

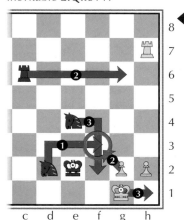

◀ 5. Karpov played **1...Nf3+**
(sacrificing the Knight to
bring out White's Pawn),
and the game ended with
the following moves: **2.gxf3
Rg6+; 3.Kh1, Nf2++.** An
alternative mate would have
been **2.Kh1, Nf2++.**

6. **1.Qe1+, Rxe1; 2.g3++**
as shown on the right. The
sacrifice of the Queen frees
the g2 Pawn, which was
pinned to the King.

Page 34 Puzzle Master Quest

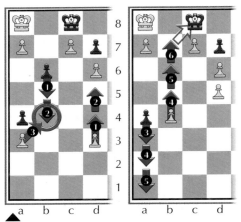

The trick to this puzzle is that the answer is forced. If you are playing White you simply cannot avoid delivering mate since, for each move, both Black and White have only one possible move: **1.d4, b5; 2.d5, b4; 3.axb4** (shown above left), **a3; 4.b5, a2; 5.b6, a1** (above right). Black can promote the a-Pawn but White has checkmate anyway with **6.b7++**. This study is by a man named Ropke, and is dubbed "The easiest problem of all".

Quest page 35

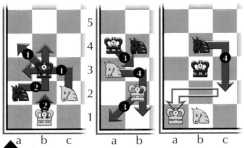

1.Na3, Ka4; 2.Kb2 (the White King has to lose a move before heading into the corner, or Black cannot set up the mating net), **Nb4; 3.Ka1, Kb3; 4.Nb1, Nc2++**. This is a classic help-mate puzzle in the sense that the pieces have to be rearranged very carefully to create the mating net for the final position.

Quest page 36

White should play **1.Bc3**. If Black replies **1...e2**, White can play **2.Bd2++**. If, however, Black's first move is **1...gxh2**, as shown below, White can mate with **2.Bxe5++**.

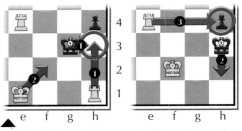

Quest page 37

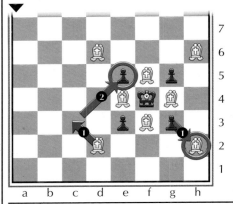

Solution a) White can play **1.Rh3**, offering the Rook. If Black accepts the sacrifice with **1...Kxh3**, then **2.Kf2** forces Black to play **2...Kh2** and White can mate with **3.Rxh4++**.

If Black declines the sacrifice with **1...Kg2** (as shown below), White can play **2.Rexh4**. Black is forced to play **2...Kg1**, and White mates with **3.Rg3++**.

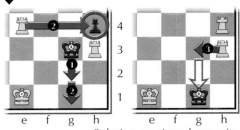

Solution continued opposite.

Quest page 37 continued

Solution b) White can play **1.Rhxh4**. Now Black has two choices: **1...Kf3** or **1...Kg2**. If **1...Kf3**, then **2.Reg4, Ke3**; **3.Rg3++**. If **1...Kg2**, then **2.Re3, Kg1**; **3.Rg3++**.

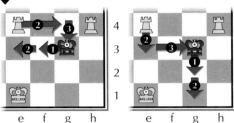

Solution c) After **1.Rexh4**, Black has the same two choices as above: **1...Kf3** or **1...Kg2**. If **1...Kf3**, then **2.Rg1, Ke3**; **3.Rg3++**. If **1...Kg2**, then **2.R(h1)h3, Kg1**; **4.Rg3++**.

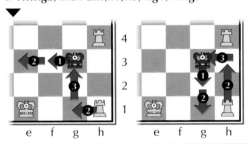

Quest page 38

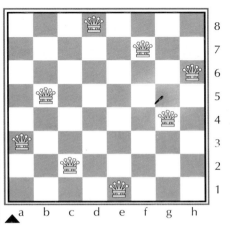

A man called Dr Nauck published all the solutions for this problem in 1850. His calculations showed that there were 92 possible variations of the basic theme of placing the Queens Knight-moves away from each other. For example, the Queens can be on a3, b5, c2, d8, e1, f7, g4 and h6.

You may have found a different solution which is fine, as long as none of the Queens is on the same rank, file or diagonal as another Queen.

Quest page 39

The Black King must be on h4. This is the square to which White can most quickly develop pieces to trap the King. To deliver mate, White plays **1.d4**, after which Black has two choices: **1...Kg4** or **1...Kh5**.

If Black moves **1...Kg4**, then **2.e4+, Kh4**; **3.g3++**, as shown below left. If Black moves **1...Kh5**, then **2.Qd3, Kg4** (or **Kh4**); **3.Qh3++**, as shown in the diagram below.

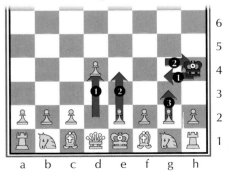

Glossary

Algebraic notation A method of recording chess moves using letters for pieces and grid references for their positions. (See page 64.)

Back rank mate Checkmate by a Queen or Rook along the eighth rank, where the King is blocked in by its own Pawns or pieces.

Castling A manoeuvre in which the King moves two squares towards the side of the board and the Rook jumps over the King. Neither piece must have moved from its starting position and there must be no pieces between them. Castling cannot take place if the King has to pass over a square that is under attack. You can castle on either the Kingside or the Queenside.

Closed file A file blocked by both Black and White Pawns.

Combination A planned series of moves that is intended to force certain responses and often leads your opponent into an undesirable position.

Discovered attack A tactic where one piece is moved to reveal an attack by another piece.

Discovered check A tactic where one piece is moved so that a piece behind it can give check.

Double check When a piece moves to put the enemy King in check, revealing a second check by a piece behind it.

Double Pawns Two Pawns of the same colour, positioned one in front of the other.

Endgame The closing stage of a game when few pieces are left on the board.

En Passant A rule which allows a Pawn to capture an enemy Pawn that has moved two squares, as though it has moved only one square.

Exchange Trading a piece for an enemy piece, or pieces, of equal value.

Fianchetto A manoeuvre where the Pawn in front of the Knight is moved one square and the Bishop is moved to the Pawn's position. From there, the Bishop controls the longest diagonal on the board and is protected by Pawns in front and on both sides.

FIDE *Fédération Internationale des Echecs.* The world chess federation.

File A column of squares running from the top of the board to the bottom. The files are lettered a–h in algebraic notation.

Fixed Pawn A Pawn whose advance is blocked by an enemy piece.

Forced move A response, usually undesirable, dictated by the opponent's previous move.

Fork A simultaneous attack on two pieces by one enemy piece.

International Grandmaster Title awarded by FIDE for consistent excellent play.

International Master A title awarded by FIDE. Lower than International Grandmaster.

Kingside Files e–h on the board.

Major piece A Queen or Rook.

Material The total value in points of a player's pieces on the board.

Material advantage Greater strength in terms of the value in points of the pieces on the board.

Material disadvantage Less strength than your opponent in terms of the total value, in points, of your pieces on the board.

Mating net Pieces working together to trap and checkmate the enemy King.

Middlegame The stage of the game after the opening and before the endgame, when most pieces are exchanged.

Minor piece A Bishop or a Knight.

Open file A file on which there are no Pawns. A file is still open even if it is occupied by pieces other than Pawns.

Opening The first stage of a game, from move one until piece development is complete.

Pawn chain A string of two or more Pawns of the same colour along a diagonal.

Pawn structure The arrangement of a player's Pawns on the board.

Perpetual check When a player is put in check repeatedly but cannot be checkmated. In this event the game is agreed drawn.

Piece Any chess piece other than the Pawn, but usually referring to a Knight or Bishop.

Piece development Moving pieces out to advantageous positions during the opening stage of the game.

Pin An attack on a piece that is shielding another piece of greater value. The pinned piece must remain in position or else expose the more valuable piece to attack.

Point value The value in points of a piece according to how powerful it is. Queen = 9 points; Rook = 5 points; Bishop = 3 points; Knight = 3 points; Pawn = 1 point; King has no point value.

Positional advantage Pieces positioned so that they have more mobility and potential than those of your opponent.

Promote a Pawn Make a Pawn into a more powerful piece (usually a Queen) when it reaches the other end of the board.

Queening square The square which a Pawn must reach in order to promote.

Queenside Files a–d on the board.

Rank A row of squares running across the board. The ranks are numbered 1–8 in algebraic notation.

Resign To admit defeat when you think your position is hopeless.

Sacrifice To give up material in the belief that this will improve your position in the short or long term.

Skewer An attack which forces a valuable piece to move and so reveals an attack on a piece of less value.

Smothered mate Checkmate with a Knight when a King is completely blocked in by its own pieces.

Stalemate A situation where the player whose turn it is next can make no legal move but is not in check. This ends the game immediately as a draw.

Underpromote Promote a Pawn to a piece other than a Queen.

Zugzwang A position where every legal move a player can make leads to a substantially worse position or defeat. It is common for a player to resign when in *zugzwang*.

Going further

If you would like to become a chess problemist, you could join The British Chess Problem Society. It publishes a magazine, *The Problemist*, six times a year. The British Chess Problem Society is open to people from any country – not just Britain. You can find out more by writing to the address on the right.

The Secretary
The British Chess Problem Society
76 Albany Drive
Herne Bay
Kent CT6 8SJ
ENGLAND

Algebraic notation

Algebraic notation records moves using letters, numbers and symbols. The ranks on the board are numbered and the files are lettered. Each piece is referred to by its initial, except for the Knight, which is N and Pawns, for which no initial is used.

A move is written using the initial of the piece and the grid reference of the square it moves to. For example, **Nh3** means the Knight moves to square h3, and **Be3** means the Bishop moves to e3. When a Pawn moves, only the grid reference of its new position is given. For example, **f4** means that a Pawn moves to f4.

Sometimes it is not clear which piece moves so in this case both the initial and file letter of the piece are given. For example, the move **Ne6** could be made by either of the Knights on the board on the right. **Nce6** indicates that the move is made by the Knight on the c-file.

The moves are numbered and White's move is always written first. If Black's move is written without White's, dots are printed after the move number, for example, **4...Ng6**.

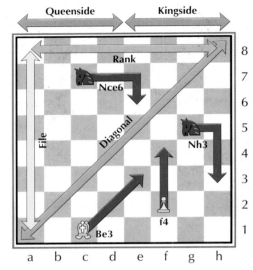

Symbols used in notation

Symbol	Example	
x	Bxh8	Bishop captures the piece on h8. (When a Pawn captures, only its file letter is given. For example, **bxc5** means that the Pawn on the b-file captures the piece on square c5.)
+	Re7+	Rook moves to e7 and puts the King in check.
++	Re7++	Rook moves to e7 and checkmates the King.
0-0		Castles Kingside (files e-h).
0-0-0		Castles Queenside (files a-d).
(Q)	a8(Q)	White Pawn reaches the eighth rank and is promoted to a Queen.
(N)	d1(N)	Black Pawn promotes to a Knight.